i

Like Snow upon Green

Stories and Poems

of childhood, youth, aging,
the effects of war,
and the constancy of love

Copyright 2020

Khotso Publishing
Peterborough, NH

Acknowledgements

I offer sincere thanks to my Fubarian friends past and present, who patiently read the work here and offered what was "good stuff" but also "needs mending stuff"; to Randall Spinks and Mark Holding who saw stories in particular poems; to editors of poetry journals who read, critiqued, and wrote letters of acceptance that brought "Cheers!" to a man in his 'golden' years; to Carl Mabbs-Zeno for his help and guidance; to my son John and Suzan, Kerri and Joe, Kristi and Danny, Amy and Nick who keep Dad / "Jack" from becoming a dull boy; and to my grandchildren Isabel and Jacob, Kira and Nora, Chloe, Logan, and Claire who bring joy to "Papa's" life.

And always, thank you to my wife Pat for space, time, and love.

This collection is for:

Peter Steele, Tim Dunn, Tim Napier and to **Gary Preston, for reading, listening, discussion and friendship.**

Table of Contents

Of You, Of Me 1

Memorial Day 2

Cold War Timeout 16

The Old Patriot 19

We're Leaving Tomorrow 21

Quiet Rooms, Quiet Life 27

For You in Our Autumn 29

Fall Back 31

Hard Love 35

A Celebration with Daisies 36

Mother and Child at the Garden 42

A Morning Wonder 43

A Child's Story 44

A Place for Waiting 45

Since That Morning 56

Something Missing 58

Veterans Day 60

The Visit 70

Like Snow Upon Green 72

A Personal Note 76

Of You, Of Me

This fire no one else feels,

this wind no one else hears.

These cold stars

in this black sky

no one but you and I see.

On this cold night of fire and wind,

and of you, of me,

this poem.

Memorial Day

On an overcast, cold and rain-threatening November morning in Cedar Park in the center of Lorrence, New Jersey, I stand in front of the Lorrence Roll of Honor, a granite monument to men and women of my hometown who made the supreme sacrifice from World War I through the Persian Gulf War. Flags billow from three silver iron poles sentried behind the Roll of Honor: the yellow and blue state flag, the black POW - MIA, and the Stars and Stripes.

But flags do not compel me to this monument. Names do. Always the names. Each name carved in granite and followed by rank, branch of service, and year of death. A former mayor's son, a minister's son, a teacher's daughter, a high school classmate I ran the roads with. Columns of names. Names that urge me to leave, run, yet stay: leave, because of their abundant numbers; stay because names are not straight and curved letters. Names are flesh. Names are not flowers and flags. Names are bone and blood, work and play, love and hate. Names are not severed hands and arms; not a shattered leg or shattered mind. Names are the clasp of a hand, an embrace of a heart, a ring upon a finger. Names are mothers, fathers, and children.

My name is Garreth Schyler (pronounced Skyler). I stay in front of the names. Never a soldier, never a sailor, Marine, or Coast Guardsman. I am the son of a soldier. I stay for the dead and the living, and for my father, a veteran World War II still alive, who returned home from the war damaged but unbroken. A cool east wind cuts across Cedar Park, slaps the three flags above me, the metal clasp of ropes ping, ca-pinging like a muted bell. Along the park's walkways benches sit empty. Lorrence's Park Street traffic passes shops, the sounds of busses and cars the same as when I grew up and came of age here, a small-town southeast of Philadelphia, west of Atlantic City, and north of the college where I avoided the draft, met my wife, and graduated. Lorrence: where my wife and I left to marry in Haven Beach on the Jersey Shore; and Lorrence, where my mother and father now live, not in the house where I grew up but in an assisted care facility.

I look again at the flags and at the names on the Roll of Honor. I think of the concentration camp my father's division liberated. He witnessed the skeletal horror the enemy committed and discarded there. He has battled the memory of it since then. He still battles it.

I remember one fight—fists our weapons. In the presence of flags and names, I recall that conflict.

*

A fair and mild Memorial Day, 1956. I was 15, an only child born one month before my father shipped out to Europe, 1942.

My mother and father and I lived with my grandparents, a situation that embarrassed me in and outside of school. All my friends lived in houses their parents owned. "Dad and I are working to save money, so that we can live in our own house someday," my mother explained to me through childhood and into my teens.

Someday hadn't happened. Not yet. Probably never would, I pondered when I watched and listened. My father was often sick: nightmares, outcries in sleep, fear of flames in the cellar's coal furnace. Periodically, Dad talked to a counselor at Colony Glen Hospital, a facility for troubled veterans, east of Lorrence; the counselor earned my father's confidence, listened to his stories, treated his post-war condition with pills and compassion, enough pills to last a month, sometimes longer. After each visit, Dad came home pale and tired, but returned to his job as a clerk at JR Heritage, a farm machinery firm north of Lorrence.

I wanted to ask my father questions. Why he backed away shoveling coal into the furnace. Why he cried out "Jimmy! Jimmy! Look out!" Why he sometimes stood with his back flat against a wall when firecrackers snapped and whistled on Fourth of July. Why?

"Don't ask him anything about those things," my mother advised me.

"But why?"

"It will only upset him. He's gone through enough."

*

Fortunately for family finances, Granddad brought home his Pennsylvania Railroad conductor's salary, and my mother worked six days a week at a women's clothing store on Park Street. "We're not rich, but we're not poor," her point of view of our 'economic situation,' one as normal to me as my grandmother's throat clicks when she "came down with a case of the nerves,"—another of my mother's explanations.

That Memorial Day of 1956 Dad was home. Home after three weeks at Colony Glen that spring. Face, arms, hands pale; voice, however, confident as a radio newscaster. I was last to arrive at the breakfast table that morning, Granddad to my right, Dad across from me. To me this Friday felt like a Saturday. I had been near the end of my freshman year at Lorrence High School the day before, and had tried to comprehend the difference between transitive and intransitive verbs; wrestled in my brain to understand a filmstrip about Hitler's rise to power. When our World History teacher explained the importance of huge stadiums and flags and music at Adolph Hitler's rallies; when he showed us another filmstrip of images of guard towers and brick buildings where there were ovens and showers in concentration camps, I remembered my father's nightmares.

I asked myself that morning, *Were those images in his dream last night? On his mind when I poured raisin bran into a cereal bowl?*

Today was a holiday, sure. More important to me, Lorrence's Babe Ruth League Opening Day. Bridge Realty, the team I played

4

on, vs. Lorrence National Bank—game one of a double-header. I'd probably start in left field and bat seventh.

Dad sipped coffee.

"I *have* to play," I told him. "You *said* I could."

"No. I *never* said you could play today, I said I'd *think* about it. I *have* thought about it. Today you're *not going* to play. It's more important—"

"It's Opening *Day*. Our first—"

"--you come to Oakmont Cemetery and pay your respects to members of this family and to soldiers who *didn't* come back. So stop your whining, Garreth, and think about somebody else instead of yourself for a change. And stop that whining! Go upstairs and get ready." He clacked his coffee cup down on the saucer. His eyes held mine as if he had caught me, a thief, in an act of thievery.

Footsteps away at the counter, Nana scraped leftover egg yolk from her plate into the sink. She clicked her throat, a sound like the tick of a clock. Her clicks now seemed in rhythm with the scrapes of her fork.

My mother said, "I'll get that, Dad," as Granddad carried his plate to the sink. He wore gray-striped navy-blue suit pants, the crease sharp as a ruler's edge. Now Granddad brushed crumbs from his undershirt as he walked in stockinged feet from the table, his steps slow, as if he considered saying something. He didn't say a word.

Resting on the back steps and damp from being watered, were three pots of red and white geraniums. I pushed away from the table, glanced at the flowers and my father's slicked-down black hair and his pale arms where black hair grew like curled weeds.

The geraniums would rest between my grandparents' feet on the Chevy's back seat floor when we made the one and a half-hour trip (grind) from Lorrence to Oakmont Cemetery in Southport, Pennsylvania. I would sit between Mom and Dad in the front seat where I had sat the year before and the year before that and the year before that and *every year before that.* The only voices heard would be theirs, not mine. They would talk about how warm it was today, how nice the green grass and flowers looked at this time of year, how nice it was to see so many flags flying. Memorial Day was, I had been taught since I was old enough to recognize the significance of flags and flowers, a day to honor and remember those in our families who had passed away in war and peace. Another day when I stood by and watched. Another day that didn't mean all that much to me.

At the sink now Nana kept her back turned to the table. She clicked her throat in what seemed like slow seconds.

Out of their sight, I heard my mother ask my father if he had called Bridge Realty manager Fran Gill.

"Yes, I called him, and yes, he understood. Now please, may I drink my coffee in peace?"

Nothing more, nothing less. Anger, frustration, and commandeering. I had heard and seen those sounds but could not tune them out for much of my life.

Until all of us left the house that morning, doors opened, doors closed. Footsteps led away and down the stairs from my room. Normal, ordinary sounds of the house until…Until.

Somewhere down Crestview Avenue firecrackers saluted the morning like wind-whipped flags.

"What was that!" my father's voice blared. "What!"

*

Southport, Pennsylvania: Nana had lived here until she married Granddad. A town 25 miles west of the Delaware River; a town known for its state college, and its close proximity for a "high speed line" service from Philadelphia; a business center of banks, insurance agencies, typical shops and narrow, red-brick homes that leaned close to cobblestone sidewalks, as if whoever lived behind the curtained and shaded windows and doors wanted little to do with those who walked by. Did kids live behind those windows, walls,

6

and doors? What was life like within those houses and yards for the mothers and fathers?

I looked at Dad's Chevy's dashboard clock: 11: 15. We wouldn't be home in time to see the last innings of Bridge Realty vs. Lorrence National Bank...

Fran Gill and assistant coach Woody Spaeth, probably at Morgan Field already... Fran in front of our dugout scoops a handful of dirt, tosses it in the air to see which way the wind's blowing...Woody in the dugout, a cigarette between his lips, slips a matchbook between his right leg and the bench, tears off a match and then strikes it, ducking his head toward the match to catch the flame...

Who'd play in left instead of me? What'd Fran say to Mom when she told him I wouldn't be there today? What'd Fran tell Woody about me? Anything about Dad?

Dad flexed his hands, slid them over and around the steering wheel. Bringing his right hand to his mouth, he cleared his throat, then put his hand back on the wheel.

He pushed his right leg against my left and said, "Don't put your knee against my leg, Garreth."

*

Oakmont Cemetery: Dad steered the Chevy past open, black, wrought iron gates. Beyond the gates the road forked. He kept to the right and followed Evergreen Way, which descended to an open plain; nothing but rows of gravestones—gray, white, pink, even black, many with American flags stabbed into the ground and waving like starred and striped hands, beside them. The graves extended perhaps a hundred yards to a wall of evergreens. A strange farm, I imagined. Nothing moved in the wind but flags and flowers and the people attending them, seeming to bow to them. Nothing lived here but grass and the visitors who walked upon it as they stood in front of names carved in stone.

I wondered: *Did flowers soon die here?*

Dad steered from Evergreen onto Haven Way, a gravel road that divided a terraced hillside on our right from the grave plots to our left. The marked areas seemed like stone-sculpted pieces of a puzzle that would never fall apart.

He parked alongside beyond a crook-shaped spigot, a metal trash barrel beside it. Ten yards away a man and woman my grandparents' age carried flowers to a gravestone. They placed the potted flowers on the ledge of the stone, stood back, and bowed their heads. Their lips moved, I heard no words.

I flexed my right hand, imagined my fingers around a baseball. I wanted spikes on my feet instead of tight black shoes. I pressed down the tips of my shoes, imagined taking a lead from first base, taking off for second, sliding in safe...

I knew my place now in front of headstones for Michael Joseph Warren and Alice Louise Warren; the son a victim of the 1920 Spanish flu epidemic, and the stillborn daughter of Nana and Granddad. I did not bow my head.

You should have, I told myself. *You didn't know Michael Joseph or Alice Louise, but they were part of your family. That means something, doesn't it?*

Maybe...

Dad now brought two trowels from the Chevy's trunk. His footsteps squish squished the pebbles He handed one trowel to Nana, the other to Granddad. They planted the geraniums, Granddad at Michael's grave, Nana at Alice's. Granddad kept his navy-blue suit coat on. Nana commented, "My, that sun is warm," as she knelt in front of the stone.

I watched their arms and hands dig, lift soil from the little holes, place the geraniums centered with the gravestones. Granddad and Nana troweled the soil around the stems, smoothed, patted, and drew their fingers away from the plants slowly, carefully to avoid, it seemed, any mistakes. Their care reminded me of the way my father planted tall zinnias and small petunias in Nana's garden at home. Stems and roots protected. Undisturbed.

"There," Nana said softly.

Granddad took her hand as, with a strained effort, she stood. They bowed their heads in front of the two gravestones.

I turned and reached into the trunk for the watering can.

Dad laid his hand on my shoulder. "I'll do it," he said without looking at me.

Granddad murmured "Hmm?" By the squint of his eyes I realized he disagreed with Dad's decision. Granddad said nothing about it.

Dad filled the can anyway. The spigot handle squeak-squeaked when he turned it off.

Granddad took the can from him without saying thank you.

"Let it go, Dad," my mother said to Granddad, not an order to him, only a wish to avoid an argument.

My father walked away toward flag-marked tombstones. His quick footsteps stomped pebbles, his arms in deliberate rhythm: one-two, one-two. I remembered his uniform hung from a beam in the attic, the khaki shirt, woolen jacket and pants still ready to be worn, if chosen.

He stopped at a veteran's grave marked by a small American flag on a foot-long peg. The flag's low right corner drooped toward the ground. Dad stood at an angle to the flag and gravestone and bowed his head. If I went to him now; if I walked quietly and stood beside him and said nothing, just stood there, would he talk to me, tell me if he knew the veteran's name? Or would he walk away toward other stones chiseled with other names?

I stood beside my mother and grandparents. I didn't move.

"Grace, I think you better go after Phil," Granddad said to my mother.

"Garreth, would you help Nana carry the other geranium?" my mother said.

Already my mother walked the path, the heels of her shoes stabbing pebbles. Already Dad was at least fifty yards away. Leaning forward like a soldier on patrol, he climbed a terraced incline overlooked by thick evergreens. Ever since I had visited here with my parents and grandparents on Memorial Day, I had never seen Dad run away. He had always stood by, his head bowed perhaps in thought of nights on watch. Maybe he recited silent prayers, maybe nothing at all. Standing before a flag-marked grave, he once had laid his hand on my shoulder and said, "Remember this, Gar."

Now I caught up to my mother. "What's wrong with Dad?"

She shook her head. Her forehead damp with perspiration, she unbuttoned her jacket and the top button of her white blouse. "Go on ahead, Gar, you're faster than I am."

I climbed the steep incline, digging in my heels as I neared the top and the dark evergreens. Beneath their boughs the air cool, a breeze through branches a long whispery sound. Here, standing on pine-needled ground, it seemed I was not in Oakmont Cemetery at all; rather, I stood within a hall lit by limb and pine needle-filtered sunlight and sounded by soft wind that carried my father's sobs, not the first not the last cries I would ever hear from him, a man alone. I heard his cries, but I did not know all the reasons for them that Memorial Day when I was young.

I know them now.

My father sat at the base of an evergreen about twenty-five yards away. His legs drawn up to his chest, his hands covered his face. Afraid of the cries that shook him, afraid of what I might see in his face, I stood still.

My mother walked slowly past me. Unafraid, she knelt beside Dad. He turned, rested his head on her shoulder. He tried to speak, but his words choked on long sobs as if he had done something wrong, lost someone or some thing dear to him. She whispered to him, smoothed her hand along the back of his neck, and then she held out her hand to me.

I knew I should go to my mother and father. I knew I should put my arms around them as I had after his nightmares. I knew they wanted me close to them now. I did not go to them. I walked away.

*

My mother and father and grandparents spoke little after we left Oakmont Cemetery; only about how nice and clean Oakmont was, how lovely all the flowers were, how busy the traffic in Southport and on highways home. My father kept both hands on the upper rim of the steering wheel, his eyes upon the road. He did not offer to let my mother drive. Home by dusk, no one said anything as we closed the car doors and climbed the front steps.

Shadows of Nana and Granddad's house leaned upon the grass and the marigolds and zinnias Dad and I had planted in the side garden. The zinnias' buds looked like miniature footballs; marigolds in bloom with yellow and orange faces like fairytale characters, but these faces had no mouth, no eyes. They were unable to look for light, and so they stood silent in the shadows.

Granddad rolled up his white shirt sleeves to his elbows and loosened his necktie. He and Nana sat on in their wicker rockers on the front porch to read yesterday's *Philadelphia Bulletin* and the latest issue of *Life*.

My mother called Fran Gill to learn the outcome of the Opening Day game. Final score: Lorrence National Bank 7; Bridge Realty 5.

What could I have done to help the team? I wondered. *Probably not much.*

You're pitching next Tuesday night," my mother added.

Upstairs Dad changed into khaki pants, white tee shirt, athletic socks and sneakers before he clipped down the stairs and strode through the dining room—His footfalls rattled china and glasses in Nana's hutch. He swung open the cellar door, yanked it shut behind him and hit the cellar stairs. In seconds I heard the thump-thump-thump, thump-thump-thump, thump-thump-thump

11

patter of the punching bag he had bought with his first paycheck from JR Heritage. As I listened, I imagined the bag flaring left and right, left and right as it rattled around against the circular metal brace attached to three ceiling beams. When Dad worked the bag, he did not like to see it hang still.

I took a deep breath, closed the cellar door behind me, and tip-toed down the steps. I sat on the next-to-last step and watched. Dad crouched facing away from me, left foot in the lead, right foot behind, and swung a tight left hook and followed with a right hook, left and right, left and right, his bare fists twirling the bag a rapid chant—boom dida boom, boom dida boom, boom dida boom.

Listening, watching, I bobbed and weaved, bobbed and weaved as he did when he ducked away from the bag only to jab with his left, jab with his right, boom dida boom, boom dida boom, a rapid percussive, addictive music. I wanted to model that rhythm.

"Can I hit?"

Flames orange and bluish-purple wavered behind the furnace grate long footsteps away from Dad, heat almost visible to both of us.

He swerved around—both arms cocked, the bag like a tossed leather ornament—and faced me. "Think you can? Come over here," he demanded.

I had hit the bag before but I could never, in spite of the ferocity and regularity of my punches, match Dad's rhythm; could never create that boom-dida-boom chant that dared me hit again.

Now I will, I told myself.

Dad drew long and deep breaths through his nostrils. His stomach pushed out and sucked in like a steady heart the front of his tee shirt, his face ruddy, his whiskers tiny black specks.

"Come on, you just gonna stand there? Hit this thing," he said. He checked the furnace, then looked back at me.

I set my feet as he had done—left toe pointed inward in line with the bag, right toe angled toward the left foot—, raised my arms, and imagined the bag as my opponent, my enemy. I bobbed my upper body, feinted a left jab and then slammed the bag with a solid right hook and careened it against the rim.

"Again," Dad said.

I bobbed back, satisfied with the force of my punch, determined to hit harder. Yes, my next punch would punish that bag. I watched it, waited until it nearly stopped swinging, and then I drove a left, countered with a right that sent the bag wobbling to the rim, not the stone-hard hit that I had wanted to give, but good enough.

Go in again. Go! Make him really watch me.

"You're telegraphing your punches," Dad said.

"What?"

"You're doing this," he said. The soles of his sneakers squeaked on the concrete floor as he stepped in front of me, feinted with his left and then drove with his right. The knuckles of his closed fist pressed—no, *knocked* against my left jaw, jarred me back, the sensation points driven by his knuckles like pulled scabs on my cheek.

Startled, I stepped back, dropped my arms. *Did you mean to do that? To hit like that,* I pleaded to ask him.

"Come on!" my father ordered. His hands beckoned me. "You gonna just *stand* there? Come *on*!"

I raised my fists, crouched.

Dad circled me, he breathed from his nostrils. He glanced at the flames behind the grate. His head bobbed like the bag when it swung like a slow clock ticking time, and he grinned. "Watch it now," he said. "Watch the left."

A trick, I thought. *A trap.*

Instead I watched his right hand, the cocked right hand that tightened in a fist, knuckles waiting to connect. Waiting to cut skin.

"Here!" He feinted a right jab, then swung a left hook that scraped and burned my right cheek, and as I crouched, as I covered the burning place with my hand he moved in on me, stood over me, his right raised to drive down on my face like a lever, his mouth a sneer. "You...I needed you...I *needed you!* You just *stood* out there like you are now. Come on. Aren't you gonna fight back? Come *on!*"

I burned to fight back, smack him. I craved to hear his yowl surprised and angered, frightened and wounded, as I felt now. I imagined myself tall and straight to meet him face to face, eye to eye. I imagined pushing him with both fists back toward the furnace, my right hand jab the left side of his face once, twice, three times—bam, bam, *bam*—the last hit a counter left that dropped him to the floor inches from the furnace.

"I didn't mean to hit you," he said. "Why'd you just stand out there in the cemetery?" Breathing hard, he still stood over me. "Didn't you see all those flags on the graves?" he said. "Didn't they *mean anything* to you?"

"Sure, I saw them. What'd you want me to do?"

"Remember the reason for the flags, damn it!"

"Okay, I *know* the reason. But why'd you take off and walk away?"

He stepped back. His shoulders slumped, his arms dropped to his sides, and his fists unclenched. "It came over me again. What I saw in the camps, what I had to do there...all of it in front of me. I couldn't help it. And I wanted you to—" He reached out his hand.

I didn't take it. "What did you do at the camps?"

He turned his back to me. He took two steps toward the furnace, the grates' slots like pulsing orange eyes. I heard him whisper. Sounds? The sounds of words? The sounds grew stronger as he made one, two steps closer to the heat, his feet spread apart as if prepared to fight.

He did not fight. He turned, faced me, then walked casually to me and extended his hand again.

I took it. His grip was tight and strong as he pulled me to my feet and put his arms around me. His body smelled sour. I did not pull away.

"I'm sorry, Garreth…I am so sorry," he said.

Guilt and anger slid out of me like blood from old wounds.

In years ahead I grew to fully understand my father and our relationship to each other. I learned that the marks on my face were wounds that belonged not only to me, not only to him, but to people he had met at the camps and knew not by name but by numbers on their arms.

Cold War Timeout

After batting practice,
shagging flies, and fielding grounders,
Uncle Lewis and I gather gear
and pedal away from the town diamond.

On the way home
Lewis pays two dimes for snow cones—
root beer his, lemon lime mine—
at old man Penn's shack,
a line drive from the railroad crossing.

"You slammed a lotta' hits today, kid,"
Lewis grins.
"Almost took my head off!"

Like him,
I grin, suck juice and ice
while the 4:10 freight train horn blares
a mile north.

Lewis squeezes his snow cone cup,

his hands hardly a ghost

wrapped around the 34-ounce slugger

that flared grounders and flies I snagged

to prove I could do it.

Pores of his acne-scarred face

weep sweat:

long-festered anxiety

after death of two sisters,

my uncle's slender six-foot frame

a crutch for his aging mother's depression.

Between the crossing gates,

the 4:10 diesel churns south,

the weight of wheels and freight

reverbs beneath our feet.

"Right on time, kid," Lewis says.

Time?

Time now a ghost of days

on diamonds of dirt and grass,

in orchards where we picked apples,

in woods where grouse flushed free,

and beat wings against sky;

on tobogganed packed snow

where we steered along hills,

all those times his hand a guide

on my shoulder,

a salve for sister and brother

and Cold War lives lost,

all for desperate prayers unanswered then

and now…

"Time to go home, kid," Lewis said.

"I'm home now," I tell him, again.

The Old Patriot

The old patriot places his hand
over his heart
and bows his head.

A parade passes.
Drums tap and roll.
Soldiers march in cadence.
The old patriot
turns away.

At a funeral
he stands while others kneel and pray.
He gazes at stained-glass saints
fixed in despair.
He studies Stations of the Cross
fixed in marble and wood,
and he weeps.
And as the flag-draped casket passes by
the old patriot places his hand over his heart,
bows his head,
closes his eyes,

and hopes guns and bombs,
rockets and missiles will cease.

But he knows better.

He knows the soldiers
will salute,
guns will salute,
and the widow's and children's hearts will break,
and all will be as it was before:
flags on porches and jacket lapels;
reports—How many wounded,
how many missing,
how many lost?

Children sit beside their mother.
They watch her receive the flag.
And he, the old patriot,
will place his hand over his heart,
touch the widow's hand,
the children's hands,
and then he will turn and walk away
toward more, more of the Past.

We're Leaving Tomorrow

The ocean breezes a cold scarf, clouds across the sun a warning. Of what, Herbert Williams was unsure. Oncoming rain? More worry about his wife Polly? After her latest round of chemo, she needed rest. A change from hospital and home to here by the ocean. Ah, the ocean's waves and warm air, to cleanse, or not to cleanse?

To cleanse?

Not so now, thought Herbert Williams, the cool wind, a different wind across his neck. The change in wind and air made the island's sunbathers collapse umbrellas, gather children and coolers, buckets and blankets, and depart the beach. Though Williams was not superstitious about such weather changes, he checked his pocket watch—4:10 this mid-August afternoon—and considered the horizon of greenish-black water and ashen sky. Time to leave.

He sifted sand from the cuffs of his trousers, slid his stockinged feet into navy blue slip-on sneakers, and returned his umbrella and chair to the rental shack. Wincing at familiar aches in his knees and legs, he gripped the railing and climbed the stairs one-at-a-time to the boardwalk.

"Aches and pains are part of growing old, sir," his physician had reported to Herbert Williams at his check-up a week ago.

"I'm certainly aware of that," Williams had said.

"No worries. Stay active. You have many good years left."

Years? If he had years, what did Polly have left? Weeks? Months?

This week on the island had been a good one for Polly. Although chemotherapy had weakened her, the island's sun and air seemed to invigorate her, though this afternoon she had stayed back at the apartment to nap instead of accompanying him to the beach.

Herbert Williams paused now on a boardwalk bench before returning to the apartment. His hands clutched the edge of the bench's wood where he sat. He watched a parade of sunbathers and sightseers, mothers and fathers and children…Tides gone by…Shells and sandcastles gone by…Tides that Jim and Dorothy, his son and daughter, had splashed and submerged in and broke through waves spouting water…Bubbly ocean water both kids carried back in buckets to the beach to bury his and Polly's legs and feet… Shells collected and brought home to decorate their bedroom windowsills…

Polly had caught him bagging the shells after both Jim and Dorothy had married and moved away. "What are you *doing*"

"Getting rid of what we don't need anymore," he said, his back to her, his voice determined.

"You will not. Give them to me. I'll keep them."

She swiped the bag from his hand. "Shame on you," Polly said.

Days later he found the bag behind her cubby of shoes in her side of the closet. He opened the bag, looked at the shells, even held one and sniffed one before he returned it to the bag. He smiled to himself as he left their bedroom.

Gone by. So much gone by. Even children. It would be nice to hear from Dorothy and Jim after he and Polly arrived home tomorrow night.

Williams pushed himself up from the bench. The ocean breeze chilled his neck. What was the current cliché? "In the best case scenario…" Yes, in the best case scenario, he and Polly would come back here next summer.

*

In five minutes he approached Wesley House, its wrap-around porch with wicker rockers remnants of the once fashionable choice of the island's summer visitors as "a nice place to stay." Wesley House's new owners had chopped and refurbished rooms into apartments, "suites" according to the brochure, the first and second floor suites for "our returning guests," the third floor "basic" rooms for college girls who worked in the island's restaurants. Gone the oriental rugs and dark mahogany furniture Williams remembered from childhood here. Gone the sliding dividers inside walls that separated the downstairs living room from the parlor. Gone the harsh-sweet aroma of pipe tobacco from the parlor and porch.

Now Williams gripped the black wrought iron railing and climbed deliberately, one step at a time, to the front porch. The outside screen door slapped shut behind him. White wicker cushioned rocking chairs empty (He hoped Polly would be waiting for him here), he walked into the reception area and took the stairs deliberately again to the second floor. He slid a metal key from the left pocket of his trousers into the lock of his and Polly's apartment.

The sitting room was all shadows and half-light. Polly had closed the curtains.

"Polly?"

He walked to the bedroom. Polly lay on the bedspread, hands at her side, her head wrapped in a white scarf. Williams listened to her breathing, smiled, and then tiptoed out of the apartment and closed the door.

Comfortable now in a white wicker chair on the front porch, he sighed and took a newspaper from a lamp table. He skimmed headlines: dangers of jellyfish in Haven City across the bay…a Strathmere bar ordered to close due to serving underage youth…More of the same, Williams thought. More of the same.

Then he heard footsteps rush down the inside stairs. Like a welcome guest Marissa, one of the college girls from the third floor, appeared before him.

"Hi, Mr. Williams."

"Well, hello there, young lady."

She was a waitress at the Danvers Hotel along the boardwalk. Tall, sun-tinted blond hair, blue eyes that made Herbert Williams smile. A nice young lady, he and Polly believed, especially since Marissa had walked with them to the boardwalk yesterday.

Many young people didn't give older folks the time of day. Marissa was not like those young people.

"Where are you off to this afternoon?" He considered politely standing for her but, not wanting to force his presence in front of her, he thought better of it. He remained seated.

"My boyfriend's picking me up. We're going out for dinner." Marissa stood at the screen door and watched traffic on the street.

"Ah…very nice. Is this a special occasion?" He immediately wanted to take back the question: *None of my business…*

"No…Just a dinner out for a change…You know how it is."

"I certainly do remember," Williams said.

He did not want to become a bore, yet he wanted to talk with her, listen to her voice, melodic almost in harmony with his daughter's voice on the phone when she said, "Hey there, Dad!"

"Did Mrs. Williams tell you we're going home tomorrow?" he asked Marissa.

Her eyes narrowing, she shook her head and then returned to check the street traffic when she said, "No, she didn't. I hope she's all right."

"Oh, thank you. She's just a bit tired. But we enjoyed your company. Anyway, it's time go home. And you? Do you miss home?"

"Mmm?" She turned back to him and said, "Oh sometimes. When I don't have anything else to do. I'm glad my boyfriend's on the island."

"How do your parents feel about your being down here?"

"Oh, they don't' mind. We email back and forth."

"I'm sure they enjoy hearing from you."

Herbert Williams wanted to stay on the porch and tell her stories of when he and Polly brought their children to the island years ago; tales of building sand castles and collecting shells; of diving into waves and feeling the ocean's power as waves tumbled and buoyed young and old alike. He wanted to share that with Marissa, ask her what she wanted for her future. She was young. She possessed a beautiful, poetic first name. She had a full life ahead of her.

But Herbert Williams stood slowly and said, "Well, I think I'll see how Mrs. Williams is feeling."

"Tell her I was asking for her."

He decided not to tell Marissa everything. "She's just tired," he said again. "You and your young man have a nice night on the town. Maybe we'll see you tomorrow morning before we leave."

"Yeah, maybe. Bye, Mr. Williams."

*

"I was *dreami*ng," said Polly Williams. Hands flat on the bedspread, her lips pale, a pink scarf around her head, she pushed herself against the pillows. "We were on the beach with the children. Then, I heard a door open. That must have been you coming in. What time is it? Come sit by me." She patted the bed's coverlet.

Herbert Williams sat beside wife, kissed her forehead, and smoothed his hand over hers.

"Almost five o'clock. How do you feel?" He kissed her cheek, cool against his lips.

"I'm all right..."

"Are you hungry?"

"Mmm, I guess. Give me a few minutes." She sighed and closed her eyes.

He patted her hand. "I left the newspaper on the porch," he said. "I'll bring it up to you. I'll be right back."

"Mmm, I guess. Give me a few minutes." She sighed and closed her eyes.

On the stairs he heard the porch screen door clack shut and Marissa's greeting in a voice and melody he had long forgotten. "Please don't go," he whispered.

From the bottom landing he stared at the empty doorway. A car door slammed, the car squealed into traffic.

Marissa was gone.

He lay his right hand on the wood railing and, sliding his hand forward and gripping the wood with each step, he walked slowly, deliberately, up the stairs.

Early tomorrow morning, he thought. We'll leave early in the morning

Quiet Rooms, Quiet Life

Art and Betty live

in the cottage-style house,

second from the corner.

Spring, summer, fall

they leave their doors open,

in case anybody wants to visit.

It's a neighborhood where families

keep to themselves.

Neighbors wave "Hey, how are ya'!"

That's all.

"They have their own lives," Art says.

Saturday mornings he follows tradition.

He brings coffee and donuts

to the kitchen table.

Together he and Betty read the town's paper

and enjoy the warm and sweet treats.

TV and radio off,

quiet rooms in a quiet house,

the way Art and Betty prefer.

When Betty finishes her donuts and coffee,

she goes upstairs.

On her way she stops

at the photographs of their children,

kisses her fingertips,

and lingers them on the faces

of Sam killed in Afghanistan,

Corlene a year later in a car crash.

"Love you, kids."

Art knows Betty's ritual.

He used to watch her

every Saturday morning.

Not anymore.

He sips coffee,

folds the newspaper,

checks the front and back doors.

No one there.

"Quiet day," he whispers.

For You in Our Autumn

I smooth my fingers across a fallen maple leaf,
one of a montage of leaves—
orange, red, yellow, and umber
upon our frost-tipped lawn.

Remember how we kicked through leaves
on our walks home with the kids?

I sweep pine needles from the deck.
Remembering those first snows of our cabined years,
I carry two Adirondack chairs inside, where, together,
we will sip warm tea
within our room of books and your paintings
of spring and summer landscapes.

Remember how we read Marlowe and Dickinson
to each other,
I your passionate shepherd,
you my lover rowing in Eden.

But I cannot ask you anymore

to whisper my name

or to swim those waters.

And so I give you prescribed daily dosage,

but those pills won't dissolve

the snakes of plaque that strangle your memory.

You stare at the television screen.

You don't smile anymore,

you don't laugh anymore

at the chummy neighbors and bumbling policemen.

Your mouth struggles for words

ordinary as a child's questions,

and your eyes wonder as an wordless infant

tries to understand faces above a crib.

And so I roam room to room,

smooth curtains, talk to photographs

of you and me and our children.

Then, together again, we watch the sunset lose

color and light beyond West Hill.

Our hill, our paths.

Remember?

Fall Back

When Margreth got into the front passenger seat of the black KIA, Ray was already tapping his fingers on the rim of the steering wheel.

"Where the hell you been?" he demanded.

She pulled the fingers of her black leather gloves one at a time, removed the gloves one at a time, stuffed them into her black leather handbag, and snapped the handbag's gold clasp shut. Semi-sweetly she said, "I'm sorry I'm late. Last-minute things, you know?"

"More like last hour things, I suppose, from the sound of your less than melodic voice."

Margreth loosened the black and white knitted scarf from around her neck and fluffed the brunette curls at the back of her head. More blunt, she added, "Just for the record, Ray? Don't be so damn belligerent."

He did not check the side or rear-view mirrors for traffic. He kept the KIA in Park.

"All right, fair enough," Ray said, "but you *know* I made dinner reservations. We're already half an hour late. They've probably given our table to somebody else. What the hell was so important you had to do?"

Margreth adjusted her position so that she looked directly at him with her back against the passenger seat and door panel.

"So now I have to account for every little minute I was late? Are you *kidding*?"

Before Ray could respond she continued: "By the way: are you going to stay in this parking space the rest of the afternoon, or are we going for drinks and dinner like we planned?"

"I was just curious about where you were, that's all."

"Curious? More than curious. Ob*sessed* is the word. I don't do *obsessed*, Ray."

Margreth turned her attention to the people exiting the circular doors from the building where she worked, the insurance company's name in gold letters between the doors and first floor windows. So many people, so many she didn't recognize.

I must be one of thousands, she thought.

She tilted her head to look at the front windows of the tenth floor; she saw only glass reflecting tops of trees in the park across the street, trees like grotesque black shadows against a sky diminishing into pale blue by the minute. Yesterday, a Sunday, the first Sunday in November, she would have had to turn the clocks back. Spring forward, fall back. It was time for fall back. Away from the glass and steel façade, she watched pedestrian traffic rush toward, rush away from them. Sitting in the front seat of this man's car, she felt small. *Here I sit, watching people on their way home or a meeting or a bar somewhere…with this man I spent the weekend with, slept with, made love with, if that's what you want to call it, for better or worse—He always finishes first.*

She sighed and asked, "So are we going or not?"

He merged into one-way, rush hour traffic.

"I was worried about you, Mar," he said, his tone, she noted, reasonable now. "I was concerned. Can you do 'concerned'?"

"Honestly worried, honestly concerned, all right, but don't interrogate me, Ray. I don't do interrogation very well. I'm not one of your small-time witnesses."

Margreth shifted her position again, now with her back against the back rest. She puffed her cheeks, blew air from her lips. "If you want to know the truth," she said, "there was a last-minute Board of Directors meeting I took minutes for. Tomorrow I'll transcribe those minutes and forward them to the company directors. That will probably take me until noon, allowing for any other little tasks that come my way. Do you want me to e-mail you my monthly calendar from now on?"

"Sure, that'd be nice. I'll send you a copy of mine, too. We'll have each other's monthly calendars. I'll superimpose a smiley face 'Have a nice day' on mine. Would you like that?"

"I'd like a drink and something to eat."

Today now, Monday morning, her back turned to him, Margreth had slept in. After they had returned from Maine, Ray had wanted her to stay with him last night; wake up with her this morning, start the work week with her, but she had begged off, told him her apartment was a mess, she was on one of those cleaning jags. Besides, it was fall, the leaves were in shades of orange and red and yellow, and she was still wearing summer clothes. She wanted to clean, organize, put away summer things, grab fall clothes out of storage. It was that time of year.

This morning river looked blackish-green to her, except for where the sun created smears of yellow and gold toward the middle. Soon that light would ripple toward shore. She thought she might walk along the river tonight, do some thinking instead of vacuuming rugs, sweep floors and bring fall skirts, dresses, and sweaters up from storage. Maybe take a day tomorrow…Then again, she could think while she worked. Whatever she decided, it would be all right. No having to explain her life to him, no listening to him explain what he wanted to do next weekend, next month, next year. No obligations except to herself. End of story.

"Take me home, Ray," she said.

"What?"

"I don't want dinner. I don't want to see you for a while. Maybe never. Take me home."

"Mar, look: I'm sorry I—"

"Don't explain yourself, Ray. I don't want to hear explanations."

"What the hell *do* you want?"

"I want to do what I want to do. So take me home."

The sidewalks were leaf-covered in her neighborhood. Streetlights and porch lights made things shine, even window box flowers still holding on before a killer frost, even the fronts of houses that still needed touch-ups to cover the flaws. She wanted now to simply stand inside her apartment and study the chairs, lamps, and end tables what she wanted to change.

No parking spaces were available in front of the apartment house where she lived. He stopped the car next to a space between two cars.

"Don't get out," she said without making eye contact him as she opened the passenger door.

She thought he might object. He didn't.

She didn't look at him as she closed the door, and she did not follow the red taillights as his car slicked over wet leaves. As Margreth walked up the front steps and took keys from her handbag, she was already thinking of a walk along the river where she could listen to the water lap the shore.

Hard Love

Where are words of natural affection?

In tremble of windows?

In tumble of flesh and bone

across wood and stone?

Where?

On paper

words appear thin as smoke,

lost as a lover's hand drawn away:

cold comfort.

The heart demands comfort hard,

truth hard as fist upon face,

as bruise upon heart.

The heart demands

your palms caress my face,

your fist no longer bruises my heart,

and your heart never break mine, again.

These are my words.

Are they enough?

A Celebration with Daisies

Jennifer stood on the porch of her house and looked up at the sky. It was as blue as her favorite blanket, her Nana's birthday present to her when she turned one. Today was Jennifer's birthday. Today she turned seven.

Small and fair, Jennifer wore a yellow polo shirt, brown corduroy pants, and white sneakers. In one hand she held the small white wicker picnic basket her mother had packed for this day, her special birthday picnic: a peanut butter and strawberry jam sandwich, crescent slices of pears, and a plastic thermos of lemonade. *"All for underneath the apple tree,"* Jennifer said to herself.

She hunched her shoulders, squeezed her arms tight, and tried to feel the blue sky come all the way down into her eyes. "Hi, Nana," Jennifer whispered.

Last week Jennifer's mother had explained to her that Nana "became very sick. Then she fell fast asleep and went to live with the angels."

It made Jennifer sad to know she wouldn't see Nana anymore.

"But you can always look at the sky and think of her," her mother had said. "Maybe Nana will be thinking of you then, too."

"I'm thinking of you, Nana," Jennifer said as she looked at the wide blue sky filled with puffy white clouds that reminded her of pillows.

Now she walked down the porch steps and into the field behind her family's white-painted garage. The field of tall grass stretched like a long wide table with forest on both sides and an apple orchard at the very end. Far beyond the orchard was the mountain. On the mountain summit was the fire tower where Jennifer's father checked the forest below for fires and helped hikers and campers obey the rules of the woods. "We have to take care of things in the woods," he had told Jennifer many times, "or else the woods won't be a happy place to be."

Jennifer was happy today as she walked the path beside the forest. She would have her picnic in the apple orchard, and maybe see Mrs. Daisy and her family. *It rained on Mrs. Daisy and her family that day Mommy and I were there,"* Jennifer remembered. *"They liked the rain but they felt sad for Mommy and me. Maybe one of the little ones will want to come home with me today."*

A breeze brushed her hair. She ran her hand along the field's tall yellow grass. She liked the way the grass felt against her skin. It was like a curtain when it blew in the wind. *Whish, whish!* the grass seemed to say. Jennifer made the sound: "Whish, whish!" It was fun talking like the grass.

It wasn't fun when she spied trash. Wadded-up napkins and two brown bottles lay at the edge of the woods. Her father had reminded her not to touch things careless people had thrown away. Jennifer used her foot to nudge the bottles closer to the trees. *'I have to tell Daddy there's litter here,"* she told herself. *"Maybe we'll come out before dark and put it in a trash bag. Then we can put it where it belongs."*

She walked on, the field on her left, the forest to her right. She looked at the blue sky again and wondered if Nana could see her. *"Maybe,"* she thought, and then, just to be sure, she whispered again, *"Hi Nana!"*

Something on the trail ahead of her caught her eye. She trotted to a cluster of new faces.

"Johnny jump-up wild flowers!"

How did you get there? I've never seen you out here, only in my friends' yards.

At the trail's edge Jennifer knelt and put down her basket close to the Johnny jump-ups.

"You look so pretty. How *are* you? I'm Jennifer. I come out here on picnics at the orchard. That's down at the end of the field. *Lots* of apple trees there. I like it because that's where the *dai*sies are, too." She patted the purple petals of one of the Johnny jump-ups. "You're so pretty…Purple and white are my favorite colors. Nana likes purple, too."

Jennifer looked at the sky again. She whispered, "See the Johnny jump-ups, Nana?"

She spoke then to the new wildflowers. "I have to go now. The daisies will think I'm not coming today. I'll come back to see you."

Jennifer lifted her basket and ran on, switching the basket from her left hand to her right so that she could brush her fingers against the tall grass at the edge of the field. "Nana, listen," she said. "Whish-whish!"

Soon she arrived at the apple orchard. She walked slowly to her favorite apple tree, the second one in the first row. She smiled at the new buds soon to become beautiful white blossoms and make her mother happy.

Jennifer used her lap as her picnic table, the scabby tree trunk for her backrest. "Old apple tree's itching my back! If I rub sideways like this it's as good as Mommy and Daddy do it."

The wind softened above her. The field quieted *whish, whish*. Everything was calm as Jennifer chewed her peanut butter and strawberry jam sandwich and sipped her lemonade. She peered at the sky again. "Hi Nana, can you see me? I can't see you but that's okay. I hope you're not sick anymore. I hope you're all better."

She put her head back against the tree and squeezed her eyes shut. Quietly she said, "I hope my Nana's all better. Please make Daddy safe, and tell Mommy I'm okay."

Jennifer opened her eyes, folded her sandwich's wrapping paper and tucked it under the thermos. She ate three slices of pears, enjoying the crunchy sound, and decided to save the last two slices for her walk home.

"It's time now," she said, tucked her picnic basket against the tree trunk, and walked to the end of the first row of apple trees.

Between the end of the row and the field she saw the white feather-like petals around a yellow face. She smiled, knelt in front of them. The daisies swayed back and forth, yet the field was hushed, and the apple limbs still.

"Hi! You look pretty today. I thought I'd come and see you, it's such a nice day. Mommy made my lunch. I just ate it underneath the old apple tree."

She sat beside the flowers and rested her fingers on the stems.

"Did I tell you about the Easter dress Mommy made for me? The same color as my polo," Jennifer patted her shoulder, "and she got me a hat to match! I wore them to church and then to Granddad's for dinner. Granddad liked it, too...

"Oh, you know what? There're some new wildflowers up on the trail. Johnny jump-ups! I don't know how they got there. They seem all alone, though, beside those big trees."

Suddenly, new sounds pierced the air. *Clip-clop, clip-clop.* A voice shouted, another voice laughed. Jennifer felt it didn't sound like a happy laugh.

She stood up and looked toward the woods.

Clip-clop, clip-clop, clip-clop.

"Who's riding out here today?" she wondered.

She heard a yell, faster tramping, a hard gallop away, and then all was quiet. Her heart pounded, and she put her hand over it.

"Who was it? Maybe they'll come back. I'll go see."

Jennifer turned to the daisies. "I'll come right back."

She ran back to the trail. She saw no one, only hoof prints in the dirt. She followed the prints along the trail. The tall grass and the trees stood still.

Studying the ground in front of her, she said, "This is where they stopped, and here's where—"

Purple and white petals lay smeared with dirt at her feet.

She lifted the petals, placed them in the palm of her hand, and gently brushed the fine dust from them.

"What happened to you? They couldn't...Oh no!"

At the trail's edge lay bent and ripped green stems and more white and purple petals. Jennifer fell to her knees and lifted the stems in her hands. "Why'd they hurt you? You didn't do anything. Why'd they have to come out here?"

Jennifer gathered all the Johnny jump-up stems and petals. She did not wipe away her tears when they fell onto the crushed petals and stems. "I'm sorry you're hurt. I'll bring you to the daisies. You'll be safe there," she said.

Wind swept through the apple trees now. The sun warmed her face. Jennifer found a stick and a flat stone near one of the tree trunks and dug a little grave beside the daisies. She scraped away pebbles and stones and picked ones she thought would make a nice border around the grave. She laid in the Johnny jump-up stems and then placed the white and purple petals at the head of the stems.

"You're all right now," Jennifer said quietly, the way her mother and Nana had comforted her after she had fallen and scraped her knee or arm. "The daisies are here. They'll take good care of you, and so will Nana."

She gently covered the wildflower Johnny jump-ups with dirt, made a small mound, smoothed the sides with her hands, and then set pebbles and stones one by one around the edge of the mound.

Her task completed, Jennifer walked slowly back to the second apple tree in the first row and picked up her basket. The wind swayed the tall grass in the field and pushed through the limbs and branches. Before she began her walk home, she looked back at the little grave.

"I know you're not happy," she said to the daisies, "but I know you'll take good care of the Johnny jump-ups. I'll come back tomorrow to see how you're doing."

Walking the path along the field, she brushed her fingers against the tall grass. The swish-swish didn't sound the same, but the sky was still blue, as blue as her mother's and father's eyes. She knew what she would tell them tonight when it was story time.

Mother and Child at the Garden

"Listen and see, my child.

See flowers in the circle,

pinks and reds and whites.

Watch them gather sunlight,

bow their petals,

and share drops of rain

as nightfall shelters them."

"Where does light go, Mother,

when there is no more light?"

"The sun will bring light tomorrow.

Light will shine through clouds.

It will shine upon the river

color the water blue and green.

"Touch the blue, dear child.

Touch the green.

Feel the colors,

and share them with the flowers.

You and your light

will return tomorrow

and keep us and hold us, forever."

A Morning Wonder

On a mild late winter morning
trees and roofs weep snowmelt.
What will become of those drops
after they fall to old snow?

Will earth accept them
at spring equinox?
Will the snowmelt nourish perennials,
or will wind and rain
wash those drops to streams and seas,
and then carry them high to clouds
so that some mild day we,
like the children our hearts sing for,
will feel them, cradle them in our hands,
and marvel at their coming again?

A Child's Story

First frost

grips the window

near where I sip steaming tea.

Were I a child,

I would tongue the glass,

savor snowflakes and stars,

feathers and lace,

ice and eyes.

Ah, what could I learn

from tasting such cold and natural secrets?

Why withered leaves cling to branches

after the fall?

Why geese take flight in a tick of time,

and what lines of lakes and light

guide their flight?

Such are the child's questions in the man.

Now, morning sun crescents a ridge miles away

and curtains the window crystal white and gold.

I touch the white,

taste the gold,

and ah, the stories to be told,

and ah, the songs to be sung!

A Place for Waiting

Before his wife died, Eben Sheldon had been a man of routine. The summer following her death Eben Sheldon changed his daily routine. "I want to get things done. Make you proud," he said to the photograph of Virginia on the living room lamp table.

He began his day before first light. Dressed in tan khaki trousers and long-sleeve beige khaki shirt, he ate breakfast and, while he sipped coffee, read the morning paper that had been tossed onto his front porch. Preferring quiet as he read, he kept the kitchen radio turned off. As Eben read, he sometimes mouthed, whispered words as if to reinforce their meaning. Afterward, he washed and rinsed the breakfast dishes, placed them in the strainer on the kitchen counter, and pushed in his chair at the table. He then was ready for his outdoor tasks.

Walking through the mud-room off the kitchen, Eben removed a single key dangling from a nail eye-level beside the back screen door. He let the screen door thack shut behind him, scuffed in his work shoes to his garage and opened the double doors, the sun warm on his neck and the aromas of metal, oil and wood as pleasant as Virginia's soft voice. From a row of garden tools arranged on hooks along one wall, he took down the three-pronged claw and the grass shears and walked to the garden in the side yard, where he loosened soil, pulled weeds and trimmed grass grown too close to marigolds, miniature roses, and tall zinnias and irises. He carried the clippings to his vegetable plot in the backyard and firmed them beneath tomato, pepper, and cucumber plants. The sun on his shoulders, Eben studied the blossoms of each plant, smiled at early fruits smaller than marbles. He watched bees hover around the tomatoes' yellow blossoms, the white of green peppers, and the yellow-orange blossoms of cucumbers, and he tried to gauge when blossoms might transform into fruits...Probably late July, early

August. Before leaving them, Eben bent closely to the plants and touched their leaves, soft as Virginia's hair, and he breathed in their aromas.

By mid-morning he heard noises from nearby yards: mothers warning children; children yelling, screeching, as they rolled and skidded on their carts and bikes; dogs yipping, barking—all irritable sounds thankfully cushioned by the wall of lilacs, forsythias, and hemlocks he and Virginia had planted the year after they bought the house, the bushes and trees pruned but now tall and wide enough as decisive borders.

"They're just kids playing," Virginia had gentled him, her hand on his shoulder, whenever he complained about the noise.

He understood children needed a place to play, but he liked—he *wanted* calm and quiet around him in and outside the house now that Virginia was gone. Two months now.

When he felt the sun glare on his neck, Eben brushed dirt from his hands, returned the garden tools to the garage, locked the doors, and sought the walls of his house again.

In the kitchen he poured himself a glass of ice water and then closed the back door and drew the curtains on the east side of the house. On the dining room wall next to the set of triple windows was Virginia's framed watercolor "Summer Irises," the one she had done two—No, three years ago after their week in Cape May. He stood in front of the painting, again, and remembered...

*

A Saturday afternoon: They had sat on a bench across the street from a church. A wedding party paraded down the church steps. Smiles and laughter, the groom holding the bride's hand as they ran down the walk, climbed into a horse-drawn carriage, and rode away waving to the guests' congratulatory cheers. "Isn't that *nice*," Virginia had said, her hand like a gift on his arm. He had agreed.

Walking back to the old Victorian style B & B where they had stayed, she pointed out purple irises at the base of a white, cross-thatched archway entrance to a yard. The next day she came back to the yard and took photographs: a close-up of the latticed entrance and a long view of the yard through the white arch. Home, she sketched the scene in pencil once, twice, and, after mixing and finding the colors she wanted, she painted the scene, the long green leaves and stalks and violet petals in a kind of attendance to the white archway, the green yard waiting. Virginia had captured the life of those images, as she had captured the stark landscaped life of "Winter Valley," the watercolor that hung in the living room: white birches and wooden fence posts in the midst of snow, ponds of snow, it seemed, with blighted grass stalks jutting through the crust; trees, posts, snow--all looming toward a distant mountain ridge. A still life, yet a life in quiet motion.

He cleared the constriction in his throat and looked away.

*

As summer continued, Eben changed his early afternoon routine. Without the need to care for Virginia, and rather than stay in the house, he took walks. He was a tall man, an inch over six feet, and in spite of his seventy-five years of age his strides were confident. He varied his route day-to-day but invariably rested on a bench in Cedar Park in the center the southern New Jersey town where he and Virginia had met, married, and stayed together forty-eight years. The park's oak and maple-shaded walkways and wooden benches provided a pleasant setting to watch the town's summer activity: traffic on Park Street, brown-skinned and white-skinned young people in their turned-around caps and baggy pants as they hustled and swaggered to whatever they listened to...Did they know where they were going? Perhaps they didn't want to go anywhere.

Perhaps they wanted to stay right there on the sidewalk and listen and swagger to their voices and music for the rest of their life.

But they must want *something*, don't they?

Perhaps. Or, he thought, he didn't understand young people at all.

47

Then again, what would Virginia remind him?

Thank goodness Dorothy and Jim, his own children, had never lacked direction. Thank goodness they had not drifted from the importance of good grades, direction, and family he and Virginia had impressed upon them. Even though Jim's medical career had taken him to California, and Dorothy preferred the dry climate of Arizona instead of the close and humid summers of southern New Jersey, they still called him once, maybe twice a month. He cherished those calls in the same way he cherished the flowers and vegetable plants in his gardens. They were something to await, to care for today and remember to care for tomorrow. Tomorrows were still important.

It surprised Eben Sheldon one September afternoon that the empty bench on which he usually rested was occupied by a man who looked the same age as he. Eben approached the bench, slowed his pace, nodded to the man, and continued on.

"Eben Sheldon?"

The man wore rimless glasses and was dressed in brown trousers, long-sleeve white shirt, cuffs folded back, and brown and white wing-tip shoes. He rose from the bench and extended his hand.

Eben did not at first recognize the stranger and was hesitant, but he accepted the man's hand.

"Henry Vandergriff," said the man.

Yes, Eben thought, as the gentleman's face, voice, and name came into focus. Here was the usher who had welcomed Virginia and him at First Methodist Church the handful of times they had attended Morning Worship...*Yes*, the gentleman who had invited them after the service to the social hour. They had accepted the invitation only once. "Too stuffy for me," Eben confided to Virginia afterwards. "Handshakes like soft bread."

"They meant well, Eben. Give them another chance sometime."

He didn't.

Now Henry Vandergriff said, "I've seen you come by here afternoons lately. Sit for a minute?"

*

He recalls his first meeting with Henry Vandergriff as timely. At home, the still window curtains and empty chairs and the closed front door had created a nearly overpowering melancholy in him, an emotion he had not fully realized until he met and began to talk with this relative stranger: a man who, like himself, was retired, lived in a house with too many rooms, some of which he did not enter for days at a time. "No reason to," Vandergriff had said during their second meeting. Eben Sheldon understood the imposing presence of empty rooms.

*

He looked forward to his afternoon meetings with Henry Vandergriff the same way he had welcomed the sound of Virginia's footsteps on the stairs when she came down to breakfast: the comfort of familiar sounds; with Henry, the comfort of unhurried conversation and silence. During autumn rain the two men shared a table at a bakery across the street from the park. They sipped coffee, talked of their past lives—marriage, jobs, travels, children. Henry and Helen Vandergriff's two sons had graduated from Lorrence High School a few years ahead of Dorothy and Jim and lived out of state, too. "You raise your kids to leave home and survive on their own," Henry Vandergriff said tapping his fingers on the table. Eben agreed, and cleared tightness in his throat.

They discussed the state of the world and its problems they could do nothing about, except "get our two cents in," as Henry put it one afternoon over coffee.

"The more you live, the more you realize there's very little you can control, so you just take care of what you have," Eben said, surprised he had articulated a point of view he had seldom expressed to anyone, only to Virginia, their conversations filled so often with daily plans and tasks.

49

He sipped his coffee. He looked at the spaces between the customers, counter spaces, Formica countertops, metal sides of napkin holders…What's it all worth?, he wondered. Things, things, things. Stuff, more stuff. Junk eventually.

Henry Vandergriff pursed his lips, scrinched one eye, and said, "The more I hear about this war over there, these suicide attacks, the more I think you're right. Where's the sense of caring for the order of things?"

Eben shook his head and restrained a smile. "Maybe only at this table," he said.

"But I *don't* understand it," Henry said. "All these years, what have we learned? First sticks and stones, then bows and arrows, muskets and rifles, now bombs and missiles. I don't understand it."

*

On a mild Indian summer afternoon, Eben accepted Henry's invitation to dinner. Henry and his wife Helen met him at their front door, where Helen thanked Eben for his gift of yellow chrysanthemums and made a place for them on the dining room table. Helen was a tall woman who wore her iron gray hair pulled back in a single long braid. She told Eben that she had seen some of Virginia's watercolors at the annual Spring Art Walk. "I could almost feel the texture of her lilies and irises," she said.

Eben stopped by the next day and gave the Vandergriffs a framed watercolor he had stored in the attic the week after Virginia had died. The painting was of a white Cape with black shutters and with lilies and irises growing beneath a set of French windows. In the lower right corner Virginia had written "Summer Hope." It was her last painting.

Before he left that afternoon, Helen said, "Come have Thanksgiving with us, Eben."

He accepted.

*

50

He recalls the days between Thanksgiving and Christmas as some of the most comfortable of his life. With his good friend he observed the people of the town prepare for holidays. As a man now watching, he thought of himself as someone who had done everything in life he had wanted to do; now, walking through Cedar Park or sitting in the bakery, he could watch others go about their lives and still feel satisfaction toward his past and present life. When you are old, he would confide to Henry Vandergriff, you better understand how things and events and people connect to each other, even if there doesn't seem to be much reason or order in the world. "There is here," Henry said, waving toward the park and the people on the street and, finally, to Eben. "There is."

*

A fine snow fell Christmas Eve day. Slow at first, it fringed rooftops and lawns and sidewalks, but by an ashen twilight the snow blew heavy and thick: a dense cloud, Eben thought, watching the storm from the Vandergriff living room window.

"They say it won't stop till tomorrow morning," Eben said.

Helen Vandergriff sat with an open book on her lap, a lace bookmark along the pages' inner seam. "We'll have to get our neighbor boy to shovel our walk tomorrow," she said to her husband who poured sherry at the dining room table.

"Nonsense," remarked Henry. "Nobody, 'specially a boy, wants to work Christmas morning."

Without turning from the window, Eben said, "I'll do it. I don't mind shoveling snow. You don't have a long sidewalk. Besides, I like being out in snow."

Later, Eben refused Henry's offer of a ride home and instead walked. He smiled in awe and appreciation of the swirl of wind and snow against him as he recalled past winter nights when he and Virginia lay in bed, their hands touching, and listened to wind whip snow against the house like sand against glass.

That night he fell asleep listening to wind and snow. He awoke Christmas morning when it was still dark. He made himself hot cocoa and then, bundled in layers and boots and hooded jacket,

51

he swept the front steps and shoveled a narrow path down the front sidewalk. The snow was well over half a foot deep, the bottom a crust of slush and ice. Carrying the shovel, he trudged the six blocks to the Vandergriff house, the windows dark; they reminded him of rectangular open mouths. He saw no lights inside. His back to the house, Eben cut into the snow at the base of the front porch. His rhythm was slow, deliberate, the only sound on the street in gray morning, the coated trees and roofs like figures in one of Virginia's paintings. He rested every few minutes, leaned on the shovel, watched his breath come from his mouth like a white ghost and heard his heartbeats kick like a dancer.

Helen opened the front door and called to him. "Eben! For heaven's sake come in and have some coffee. Our neighbor boy's coming over in a little while. He'll do the rest. Come on in," she said, almost pleading.

He waved and replied, "In a minute."

He turned away and cut the next block of snow. At the corners of his eyes burst bright waves of light. Thinking it was sunlight glaring off the snow, he looked at the sky but it was still low and gray. His breath came shorter. He thought it strange because he had not scooped the snow, and now he felt perspiration trickle down his face and inside his undershirt. His heart felt clamped in a vice.

Then, he collapsed.

*

Eben Sheldon often speaks of his recuperation in the hospital and at the Vandergriff home as a lifeless period, an experience like none other in his life. His area of existence was a confining place, brightened only by flowers and voices outside the rooms. Yet, he saw these comforts as entities of a greater loss, but even as he regained strength to climb stairs, walk around the block, and eventually take care of himself at home, he looked upon such activities as less than ordinary, wastes of time, and he yielded to waiting.

Without his knowing, the Vandergriffs notified his son and daughter of his illness. Jim could not take leave from his practice until the spring. He requested weekly updates from the Vandergriffs.

Eben called him the night Helen and Henry brought him back to his house.

"How are you, Dad? It's good to hear from you," his son said.

"As good as can be expected with this sort of thing, I guess. I'm home, and it looks like I'm going to be here for a while."

"Well, that's good. Listen, I'm sorry that…"

Eben paid little attention to his son's apology. The tone of Jim's voice was like the color and texture of woodwork around Eben's front door: smooth, defined, clear-grained. You could pass it by without seeing it and yet remember how it was and how it felt when you first ran your hand across it.

"…as soon as I can get away," Jim said.

"I expect to be here," Eben said.

Of Dorothy's appearance in his front doorway, Eben says he did not recognize her at first. The sun bright through the windows and door made her a silhouette. When she said "Hi, Dad," he immediately recognized her voice, and as she stepped closer he saw that her blond hair looked hard and tinted the way some nurses colored their hair, and she held her mouth in a grudging smile.

Dorothy set her suitcase of the living room rug and took his hand.

*

At the breakfast table the next morning she poured tea for him and for herself. She set his cup and saucer in front of him. "There you are," she said, but something in her tone annoyed him, reminded him of the condescending nurses who had assumed he was deaf when they greeted him: "How are we today, Mr. Sheldon?" they shouted; he shouted back, "Good enough to hear you!"

Dorothy sat across the table from him now. "Dad, you trust me, don't you? I mean, if I were to do something that involved you, you'd know I would be doing it for the best, wouldn't you?" She sat back and curled her arm around the top left spindle of the chair.

53

"I think I know what's coming next," Eben said, "and the answer is 'No.' *No!*"

"That's what I thought you'd say. But—"

"Don't treat me like one of your clients, Dorothy. I'm not moving to some place I don't know anything about and don't *want* to know anything about."

"Dad, listen: I can easily find a living arrangement for you close to where I live. It would be your own place, you could take care of it the way you want, nobody looking over your shoulder and telling you what to do. Not even me," she smiled. "Nice neighbors. *And*, a healthy climate..."

"Dorothy?" he said, and held up his left hand to stop her. "No."

He wrapped his hands around the mug of tea and bent over and slowly brought the mug to his mouth. He felt the warmth of the tea on his lips before he sipped it.

She looked at the cabinets and the floor and smiled.

Days passed. He read the newspapers she brought home from the supermarket. They watched TV together after dinner, talked about the fighting in Iraq. "Wheels within wheels, fires within fires," he said. "Nothing seems to change. I don't understand it."

"Neither do I, Dad," Dorothy said.

She restocked his refrigerator and kitchen cabinets. He heard doors push open and snap close, and after she went upstairs one morning he heard the vacuum whir over the floors and carpets in the rooms he had not opened in weeks, maybe months. He opened the door to the mud-room, took his jacket from a peg, slipped it on, and walked through the house to the front door.

Dorothy came down the stairs. "Dad?"

"I'm just going to stand on the front porch, for god's sake."

Feeling her eyes on his back, he controlled an urge to slam the door.

The day was bright. Sunlight glinted off the snow, and the snowmelt dripped from the edge of the roof. The scents of water and snow and something else—Grass, dirt? No, too early—drifted in the air. The sidewalk path that Dorothy had cleared was not as wide as the space he would have made. One block away the mailman bent toward the front steps of a house.

A still life, he thought, but one with quiet motion.

Eben telephoned Henry Vandergriff when he went back inside. "Come on over here," he said.

*

He says that Dorothy understood his reasons for wanting to stay. The day she left to fly back to Phoenix she said, "I'll worry about you," and then put her hand on his arm and kissed him.

"That's your prerogative," he said. Then: "Tell your brother I'm all right."

"I'll tell him more than that." She hugged her father and, keeping her arms around him, said, "I'll call you when I get home."

He says the house seemed suddenly quiet and neat; too quiet, too neat, after Dorothy left. He found newspapers stacked in a recycle bin in the shed off the kitchen, and the lamps and end tables appeared angled differently, closer to the chairs than he wanted them to be. He smiled, and re-adjusted their position.

In the living room he looked again at Virginia's painting "Winter Valley," at the snow that, even in stillness, seemed to move toward the mountain, and he thought how right and natural is that journey.

Since That Morning

Since that morning
of smoke and ash
upon high blue sky,
he walks the path
along the brook,
and watches white water
whirl across stones,
current fast as fire.

And since that morning,
he finds a hill where he stands
sure of distance
between mountain and sun,
first star and moon,
horizon and home;
yet, distance and perspective,
as in memory,
change as smoke and ash
drift in cries of love betrayed
by secretaries and presidents.

The pull of the moon

the turn of the earth,

the questions above the coffins

draw him near,

yet far from home.

Something Missing

A warm night,
air still as cold wood.
He watches porch and window lights
of neighborhood houses.
The lights do not shimmer;
they stare
at him,
at neighbors' houses,
but to him, always, it seems,
at him.

He knows rooms of those windows,
names of husbands, wives, and children
who live, laugh and argue in them.
He has seen graduation and wedding pictures,
shaken hands and sipped drinks at parties,
nodded agreeably at opinions and statements
about the neighborhood, the town—
indeed, society.

Not close friends,
not mere acquaintances;
they are neighborhood friends,

driveways and hedges the fences
friends don't need.

Yet, something is missing.
Not snow, not ice, not sunlight.

Will the center of family and friendship hold?
Or will lives drift into apathy, break,
and fall apart like broken toys and promises?

The cold hard light of stars:
He feels it touch him,
and the windows and walls
of those houses.

Where will that light lead?
Will friends be open to the wonder of it,
seek its beginnings and history?
Or, will they turn their backs,
repeat indifference,
and cast hard eyes
upon a beast that slowly, slowly,
will find its prey and descend upon them?

Veterans Day

On this fall morning at ten o'clock, my son Dan beside me in full-dress United States Army uniform, I sign out my parents from Shelborne Place, the assisted living facility their home for the past two years in Lorrence, New Jersey. I tell the resident supervisor that Dan and I will bring them back and join them in time for noon lunch. An aide helps Dan and me assist my mother from her wheelchair into the back seat of my Ford Focus, my father from his chair into the front passenger seat. Dan and I fold and stash the two wheelchairs in the trunk.

Today is the first time since Dan enlisted and moved away that he has seen his grandparents. He sits beside my mother and pats her arm.

"Don't you look nice in your uniform," my mother compliments him. "What are all those decorations for?"

He explains the bars and ribbons (my son a patient teacher) as I turn onto Lorrence's North Park Street for the one-mile ride into the center of town. In the rearview mirror I see my mother concentrate, silently mouth some of Dan's words as if to impress his information upon her memory.

I glance at my father, Philip Schyler: War II veteran. Father. Grandfather. Damaged by skeletal bodies he saw in mass graves: haunted by recurring nightmares. The stiff, upturned collar of his topcoat partially hides his lower jaw, the bill of the army cap Dan gave him like a wing over his upper forehead. His mouth open, he breathes as if he is ready for a walking race.

North Park Street: the landscape of lawns, law offices, insurance agencies, two churches, older homes—becomes familiar to my parents. My father straightens his shoulders. He utters a sound that affirms his interest, his wonder of the neighborhood of the southern New Jersey town of Lorrence where, over fifty years ago, he was on a first-name basis with the owners of these homes and offices.

I stop for the red light at the Park Street - Crosstown Avenue intersection. The Methodist Church presides on the far-right corner.

I ask, "Dad, there's the Methodist Church. That's where you and Mom were married."

He responds, "Nnh," and tilts his head back as if to refer to my mother.

"All that red brick. It looks like a school instead of a church," she observes. "A shame when they tore down all that white wood."

"How many years have you and Mom been married, Dad?"

"He can't tell you anymore, Garreth," my mother says.

"I just wanted to ask him."

"Sixty-three," she says flatly.

Except for the post office and banks, most businesses are open. Doors and windows display American flags; red, white, and blue-lettered signs hawk Veterans Day sales. Icicle style lights blink in a gift shop window.

Two blocks later, at the Park Street – Lorrence Avenue red light we are first in line. Diagonally left of the intersection people stream across the grounds and walkways of Cedar Park. A white banner strung from two oak tree branches proclaims in bold red 'Welcome Veterans!' above the park's Lorrence Avenue entrance. I crack my window an inch. A band's brass and percussion rouse the spring air from a distance.

Her voice now of amazement, my mother asks, "Is *that* where you're bringing us?"

But she and my father do not need Dan and my assertions to know our destination is Cedar Park. Here, on a September 1945 morning, my mother wheeled me in a stroller; in the midst of a shoulder-to-shoulder, flag-waving crowd, she held me tightly by the hand the day Lorrence celebrated the end of World War II.

Now she marvels, "*Look* at all those people!"

I park two spaces down from the bank where my father began duties as a teller, spring 1955. While I press the trunk-release button inside the glove compartment, Dan jumps out, lifts the trunk's lid, and removes the two wheelchairs. He guides one to the front passenger door, the other to the rear door. One arm around his back, the other under his arm, I ease my father onto his wheelchair's padded seat; Dan guides his grandmother into hers.

I lean beside my father. From beneath the bill of his cap, he peers at me certain of who I am and in decisive expectation of an event he cannot name anymore but will not bring him harm. He blinks, the corners of his mouth twitch toward a smile. He understands me; his understanding affirms in me that the four of us are right in being in this park on this morning for this ceremony.

Many years ago in a cemetery on a Memorial Day, in fear of my father's tears of anguish, I had turned away from his and my mother's outstretched hands. Now, as I wheel him to Cedar Park, I place my right hand on the shoulder of his coat. I am grateful to bring him to this ceremony and to offer him my hand and arms.

Dan and I position ourselves at the walkway's entrance to the Lorrence Roll of Honor: veterans' names carved in a granite monument, each name supported by the veteran's branch of service, the war in which he or she served, and date of death. Above this monument, the Stars and Stripes, the State of New Jersey flag, and the black MIA - POW hang still. On both sides of the walkway people hold bouquets, single flowers, and small American flags. The American Legion band plays a mournful hymn arrangement of "America the Beautiful."

The sky suspends ashen gray.

Behind a podium, mere footsteps in front of the Roll of Honor stand two men and one woman: a bald, brown-mustached man in a gray three-piece business suit; a woman in a navy blue raincoat and who now turns to speak to the bald gentleman; and, a shorter, white-helmeted American Legion-uniformed man who stands at ease.

I kneel next to my father. "How you doing, Dad?"

"I think he's cold," my mother says.

I place my palm against his cheek. He nods, trembles a smile. "He's fine, Mom."

A silence threads through the audience and encloses us.

Traffic whirs on Park Street. The woman in the navy-blue raincoat steps to the podium; her black-gloved hands rest on the raised sides. She raises the staff of a cordless microphone fixed to the podium and introduces herself by name and title: Sheila Herbert, Mayor of Lorrence.

"Thank you all for joining us here this morning on this Veterans Day remembrance," she offers with visibly natural sincerity. "I welcome all of you to our ceremony. A particular special welcome, also, to the Lorrence veterans here today and to veterans visiting us from other communities. We are grateful for your service and honored by your presence."

Turning to the business-suited man, she introduces him as Lorrence's First Presbyterian Church minister, "who will offer the invocation."

I place my hands on my father's shoulders, his coat bulky beneath my hands; my own flesh unable to sense flesh and bone through the thick cloth of coat and sweater; I imagine bones brittle and thin and pale but connected, somehow, to a single substantial heart and mind.

Dan smiles at me, nods as if he affirms that heart and mind.

"...to make us mindful of the needs of others," the minister offers, "and to share in the coming days the generous fellowship represented by this gathering, through your mercy. Amen."

"Amen," the crowd, except for Dan and me, responds.

I scan the crowd: heads bowed, eyes apparently unto some place within; lined faces I do not recognize. The flags wave in the wind as a slow pulse.

The mayor next introduces the Legion-uniformed retired master sergeant, who leads the crowd in the Pledge of Allegiance.

How easy to place hands over hearts, I remind myself. How easy to speak like a long-absent Grace, the words in near unison. Dan's voice carries the command of an order given. My mother speaks a syllable or two behind everyone else; her gloved hand lays limp upon her tan topcoat. My father stares at the flags as if in prayer. His lips move; no words come forth. His right hand wavers upon the place where his coat shelters his heart. I bow my head.

Dan removes his right hand from the medals and ribbons on his jacket and places his hand upon his grandfather's shoulder.

"Dad's cold, Garreth," my mother warns me again.

"He'll be all right," I tell her. "He wants to be here."

"I know, but—"

The mayor leans to the microphone. She announces, "Now everyone, I'd like to introduce our guest speaker: Mr. Woody Spaeth."

Accompanied by strong applause, a black-suited man, the left sleeve of his jacket tucked inside the left pocket, steps from the rope of people in front of the Roll of Honor and, somewhat bent-kneed, approaches the podium. He shakes hands with the three principals at the podium, and then he greets us, his audience: "Mornin', ever'body. S'cuse me while I take care've some business here first."

The assistant coach of the Babe Ruth League team I played for; the former soldier who lost his left arm to a Nazi machine gun attack; the man whom my father challenged with a screwdriver when our team manager removed me from the pitcher's mound; the man whose black '51 Mercury my team and I dreamed of owning: Woody Spaeth.

He removes a folded paper from the right-hand pocket of his suit coat; next, a pair of reading glasses from his shirt pocket. Left stem, right stem, he hooks them behind his ears, then smooths the paper upon the podium.

I whisper to Dad, "Remember Woody?"

Dad wheezes. His eyes film. He nods, at what? Memory of skeletal bodies in mass graves? A man he once shared playing dirt infields and green outfields with? The convergence of Past with Present?

I close my father's topcoat collar to protect his throat.

"Unaccustomed as I am to public speaking," Woody begins, and we and his audience chuckle. "I'm sure you know that by now…"

My former coach, like my father, approaches 82 years of age. How different, though, these two men, not only different physical statures and capabilities but how they recovered, or didn't fully recover, from the war they survived. Yet, through losses, retreats, and gains, these men are survivors. They are alive. They are here.

Woody's voice sounds withdrawn, tight. He pauses, peers at his notes and then raises his right hand in our direction. Almost to himself, he says, "There he is, everyone."

The crowd follows the lead of his hand to my father.

"A lot of veterans I'd like to acknowledge, but one gentleman's here I haven't seen in a long time. Too long. Many of you may know him: Phil Schyler.

"I won't go into detail about the war Phil and I fought. The names on the Roll of Honor behind me say enough about that and other wars, past and present. I'd like to say something about what it means to be a soldier. Phil Schyler was, and is, a good soldier.

"A good soldier puts on a uniform and lives in that uniform for the rest of his life. Even after he comes home; even after he takes it off and hangs it up, he lives in that uniform. Army, Marine, Navy, Air Force, Coast Guard, he's always a soldier. Men, women—

we go to work, do our jobs, and take care of our family the best we can. Do the best we can at everything we undertake. You know what I'm talking about.

"It's not easy. Things we saw and never want to see again, they stay with us. They did with me, they did with Phil Schyler, and they did with a lot of you vets here. It's tough living with the memory of a guy hunkered next to you shot to hell.

"But a good soldier lives through it best he can. He goes on. That's what you vets here did while our families at home did the best they could. And that's what Phil Schyler did. With the help of his family, and with the help of all our families, we lived through it the best we could.

"Phil and all the other soldiers here deserve our thanks."

I do not look at Woody as he pats the podium; and, though I hear the encompassing wave of applause, I do not look at the crowd that encloses us. I look at my mother, who wipes her eyes. I look at Dan, his hand a recognition and tribute upon his grandfather's shoulder.

"We have Lorrence's Roll of Honor behind me here," Woody continues, "and we have our flags right up there. We know what they stand for. But in my opinion, for what it's worth, they aren't enough for what men and women fought and died for and are *still* fighting and dying for. Damnit, there's gotta be more to show for what veterans do. I don't know what the hell that something more is, but I hope someday somebody'll figure it out.

"Thanks again for coming here today."

Applause swells like gradual and gentle waves and accompanies Woody as he walks to us.

He greets my mother first. He bends, takes her hand, and kisses her cheek. Then, directly in front of my father, Woody stands at attention, salutes him, bends down, shakes my father's hand, and lays his arm around his shoulders.

"An honor to have you here and see you again, Corporal," he says.

Dad does not immediately relinquish Woody's hand. When Woody does withdraw, Dad's fingers remain momentarily on the back of Woody's hand.

"Hey there, Gar." Woody's right hand feels narrow in mine, its bones and tendons more firm than Dad's. Standing beside me, shifting his weight right and left, he looks like an old fighter uncomfortable in a suit.

I introduce him to Dan.

"An honor, sir," Woody salutes him.

"Likewise, sir."

We watch the mayor introduce the daughter and son of a pilot from Lorrence killed in action during the Persian Gulf War. The girl and boy lay wreaths on the ground in front of the Roll of Honor. From the moment the girl and boy first carry their wreaths to when they return to their places, Dan and Woody salute them.

From behind the monuments a voice barks, "*Pre-sent, arms!*"

Slaps of hands upon rifle stocks.

"Ready, arms!"

Clicks.

"Fire!"

My father falls forward. Dan, Woody, and I hold him, cradle him as the guns salute again and again. He breathes and whimpers as if he has run a course. We wrap our arms around him.

Dan pats my father on the back, and whispers, "It's okay, Granddad. It's all right."

The guns fall silent. Smoke rises, tendrils toward the branches of trees, and the flags move as if to unfold but instead curl in upon themselves. "We shouldn't have come here, Garreth," my mother says. "It's too much for Dad." Dan, Woody, and I help my father settle again, his back against the wheelchair's leather padding.

I do not to reply to my mother but I lay my hand on the arm of her overcoat. Then, as comfortably as I can I tell her, "Mom, he'll be all right. I promise." I pat her twice on the arm. She bows her head. She nods.

Then, the singular melody of "Taps" calls across the park. A melody we have heard too many times in films, at memorial services, at presidential funerals. It is the same trumpeted call, the same trumpeted answer, but today with troubling finality. I can articulate reasons for explorations past and present, for broken treaties, even reasons for political assassinations and causes of war. However, I cannot comprehend, nor can I articulate why one human being drives an explosive-loaded truck into a market place, café, school…any location where men, women, children go about their daily lives. Such an act is chaos, and after chaos the horrific absence of words, and without words we cannot interpret what we have lost. Therefore, we die.

The Presbyterian minister's Benediction, though well meant, speaks a simple platitude: a hope of "light in which people may see your good works, and be thankful in the comfort of each other. God bless you all, and thank you," the all-too-familiar and hopeless refrain of presidents whose unstudied decisions lead us toward chaos.

I am frightened. Suddenly frightened at the sight of people streaming back through the park. Their duty done? At the sight of the flags that move like stiff gowns against the pole in the gentle wind; at the sight of soldiers and civilians who stand in respect and who lay flowers at the base of the two monuments. *What more? How many more?*

By the time the band folds up chairs and snaps instruments into boxes, few people remain in front of the names in the monument. They read names, bow their heads, place flowers on the ground, and walk away. The sky remains the color of destroyers and air-craft carriers.

My father makes a straining sound in his throat. "There!" he demands.

I kneel beside him. He does not look at me. He points toward the Roll of Honor with his trembling left hand as if its own mind and blood have found a wondrous discovery. He regards me with the most prayerful expression I have ever seen from him. "Uh'there," he begs.

I push him slowly forward to where he can see the Roll of Honor's names. Dan and Woody follow with my mother.

My father strains again from the back of his throat: "Up!"

"I'm not so sure," my mother cautions.

Already Dan is at Dad's left side, I on his right. Together we lift him from under his arms to his feet. His knees buckle. Our arms around his back sustain him and, as if he knows the drill, my father places his left arm across Dan's shoulder, his right arm across mine.

"You can do this, Dad," I tell him.

Lifting, holding, Dan and I bring my father face to face with the Roll of Honor.

Name to name. His name is not there. Not yet.

My son takes my father's arm and places the palm of his grandfather's hand upon the granite.

Philip Schyler's face is of fear and love, sorrow and joy; emotions that enwrap themselves around us as we hold him at his town's tribute. There, his shoulders shake, his knees buckle again, and his body hangs between Dan and me. My father weeps.

The sounds he makes seem gasps for air but strong and clear enough to utter one word: "*Yes.*"

The Visit

Jesus stopped by yesterday.
He looked the same
as when we first met:
long brown hair, beard, white robe, sandals.
A gentle, soft-spoken man.

He was thirsty.
I gave him water.
He was tired.
I offered a chair.

He spoke:
"Things have not changed
since I began my mission.
I gave you land.
You carved craters and trenches,
you filled them with skulls and bones.
I offered rivers and seas.
You floated caskets of oil and flesh.
I gave sky.
You lifted satellites and missiles.
I blessed you with children.

You taught them grenades and guns.
You severed hands, cut out tongues.
There are too many bodies in the earth,
too many bones in the sand,
and moneychangers have returned
to the Temple.
These acts were of desecration.

"Are we at an end of things?" I asked.

"I have given my life.
I cannot give more."

He held out his hands.
The lines and scars were the same as mine.

Like Snow Upon Green

1944

The siren wailed only once,

then fell silent.

The boy's mother and father

darkened all lights,

closed all curtains,

and pulled down all window shades in the house.

"I'll be back soon," the father said

as he left their house,

and closed the door behind him.

The mother cuddled the boy

in the living room

dark as the boy's nightmares.

He did not cry as he asked,

"Why did Dad leave?"

"He has to check other houses

to be sure no lights are on."

"Why?"

"So enemy planes won't see us."

1950

In a passenger train car

the boy sat beside his mother again.

In front of them a man held a newspaper:
The headline read,

TRUMAN SENDS TROOPS TO KOREA.

The boy asked, "Are we going to fight
in Korea?
"I'm afraid so," his mother said.
"Will Dad have to go?"
"No."

1954

The boy, now 13, listened to morning news
on the radio.
A newscaster reported civil war
in French Indo-China and a long battle
at a place called Dien Bien Phu.
Many French soldiers were killed.
The boy wondered,
Will American soldiers have to fight
at Dien Bien Phu someday?

1964

On a beach that summer
the boy, now a young man,
wondered why Buddhist monks
intentionally immolated themselves.
A month later he read that U.S. naval vessels

were fired upon in the Gulf of Tonkin.

"It's coming at us," he said to no one.

1967

Visiting his parents one weekend,

the young man saw a black sedan stop

in front of the house next door.

Two soldiers and a minister got out of the car

and walked to the front door.

"It's here," the young man quietly said.

"What did you say?" his father asked.

"The war's next door now."

To himself, the young man said,

"But we knew that all along,

didn't we."

2005

In the fall, the man, now a father,

read his son's e-mail from Iraq.

"Black smoke in the sky adds ambiance

to this place," his son wrote.

That December the man's son returned home.

The Present

Memorial Day weekend:

The man and his wife and son visit Arlington.

They stand beneath a tree.

"The white crosses, so many. So, so many,

like rows of snow upon grass.

The rows end and begin again

like war always pursuing us. Always.

But we know that, don't we.

We've always known that.

Or have we?"

A Personal Note

You may wonder about the sources of stories and poems in this collection. Sometimes I wonder, too. I wonder about figurative and literal avenues and homes, the woods and streams and baseball diamonds where, in their particular way, the poems and stories here began life.

Radio nourished that life. Radio sparked my imagination. As a child I listened and imagined. I visualized Don MacNeil's "The Breakfast Club." My lively and understanding mother and I marched around our breakfast table. Afternoons I visualized Sergeant Preston of the Northwest Mounted Police as he and wonder dog Yukon King ("On King, on you huskies!") faced challenges of the Yukon and brought lawbreakers to justice. So did John Reid, aka. *The Lone Ranger*, in the Far West. So did Lamont Cranston, aka. *The Shadow.*

What did I gain from these and other radio dramas? The rewards of the human imagination. Creativity. The announcers' voices introduced adventures: the sounds of hoof beats and gunshots; sounds of wind and dogsleds pushing through snow; the menacing laugh that chilled my scalp as The Shadow menaced Evil that lurked in the hearts of men. Perhaps most of all I gained variations of rhythm and the pace of a story.

Television: The black and white television screen in my parents' home did not prevent me from radio. I did not forsake the drama of "Gangbusters" and "Gunsmoke," nor Red Skelton's comical two seagulls Heathcliff and Gertrude on his show." The police and Matt Dillon still brought lawbreakers to justice. And television's golden age introduced me to live drama via Playhouse 90, where I watched Jason Robards portray Hemingway's hero Robert Jordan in *For Whom the Bell Tolls.*

Radio and television remain my friends. So do movies. So does live theatre. All of them talk to me in distinct voices in distinct settings. They dramatize scenes that, after I turn off Power or after I leave the theatre, my imagination thrives with scenes, dialogue, and music; film soundtracks, for example Elmer Bernstein's music for "To Kill a Mockingbird" and Burt Bacharach's "What's New Pussycat" underscore the stories and mirror the drama and comedy. Scenes and voices that drifted me off to sleep in my youth still reside there and remain inspirations to me. Stephen Sondheim's "Move On," from *Sunday in the Park with George* has become a personal anthem.

Though I did not forsake radio and television, nor films and plays, I moved on from them to books. From Shakespeare to William Butler Yeats; from Emily Dickenson to Donald Hall and Sharon Olds; from John O'Hara to John Updike; from Thomas Williams to Ernest Hebert and Robert Olmstead. I've been there, and I'll go back there again. Why? I like what they and how they say it.

Except for "A Celebration of Daisies" originally composed in Pitman, New Jersey 1963, the other stories and poems here were written in Keene, New Hampshire. Inspirations? Childhood, September 11, 2001, my son enlisting in the Army and, thankfully, surviving two tours in Afghanistan, two in Iraq; and, awareness of the rhythms and passages of life. Over decades the poems and stories have endured revisions in word and deed, even grammar. Through additions and deletions, the characters continue to experience challenges within themselves and family. The young, the middle aged, and the elderly reach out to others. Herbert Williams, Eben Sheldon, and Philip Schyler want the touch of recognition. They, indeed like us, want and *need* to be held.

Also by Jack Hitchner

Not Far From Here: flash fiction and poetry
    (Scars Publications)

Seasons and Shadows: a chapbook of poems
    (Finishingline Press)

How Far Away, How Near: short stories
    (Amazon Kindle)

The Acolyte: a novel
    (Amazon Createspace)

Pieces of Life Between Latitudes: poems
    (Encircle Publications)

Credits

The Aurorean, published by Encircle Publications, Farmington, Maine

The Avocet, edited and published by Charles Portolano, Fountain Hills, Arizona

Clark Street Review, edited and published by Ray Foreman, Berthoud, Colorado

Pieces of Life Between Latitudes: Encircle Publications

Evening Street Review, published by Evening Street Press, Sacramento, California

Cover: Jack Hitchner